HAPPY BIRTHDAY, SAUSAGE!

MICHAELA MORGAN
ILLUSTRATED BY FELICITY SHELDON

D0230455

BLOOMSBURY EDUCATION

LONDON OXFORD NEW YORK NEW DELHI SYDNEY

BLOOMSBURY EDUCATION
Bloomsbury Publishing Plc
50 Bedford Square, London, WC1B 3DP, UK

BLOOMSBURY, BLOOMSBURY EDUCATION and the Diana logo are
trademarks of Bloomsbury Publishing Plc

First published in Great Britain in 2010 by A & C Black, an imprint of Bloomsbury Publishing Plc

This edition published in Great Britain in 2019 by Bloomsbury Publishing plc
Text copyright © Michaela Morgan, 2010
Illustrations copyright © Felicity Sheldon, 2019

Michaela Morgan and Felicity Sheldon have asserted their rights under the Copyright,
Designs and Patents Act, 1988, to be identified as Author and Illustrator of this work

This is a work of fiction. Names and characters are the product of the author's imagination and
any resemblance to actual persons, living or dead, is entirely coincidental.

All rights reserved. No part of this publication may be reproduced or transmitted in any form or
by any means, electronic or mechanical, including photocopying, recording, or any information
storage or retrieval system, without prior permission in writing from the publishers.

A catalogue record for this book is available from the British Library

ISBN: PB: 978-1-4729-5963-8; ePDF: 978-1-4729-5964-5; ePub: 978-1-4729-5965-2;
enhanced ePub: 978-1-4729-6948-4

2 4 6 8 10 9 7 5 3 1

Printed and bound in China by Leo Paper Products

MIX
Paper from
responsible sources
FSC® C020056

All papers used by Bloomsbury Publishing Plc are natural, recyclable products from wood grown
in well managed forests. The manufacturing processes conform to the environmental regulations of
the country of origin.

To find out more about our authors and books visit www.bloomsbury.com
and sign up for our newsletters

Chapter One

Would you like to meet a plump
and playful, loyal and loving,
lovely, little long dog?
Here he is...

He looks a bit like a sausage.
His favourite food is... sausages.
And his friends and family call him...
guess what?

Sausage!

Fitz and Spatz, the two snooty cats, share his home. But they don't really like sharing.
And so they don't really like Sausage. They call him…

Silly Sausage!

The cats are never kind to Sausage.
Sometimes they *pretend* to be kind…

but really they just like to make fun of him.

Sausage has lived with his family for nearly one whole year. Here they are:

Gran

Elly

Hammy

Jack

And what a year it has been!

January
February
March
April
May
June
July
August
September
October
November
December

Sausage arrives.

Sleepover at the Spooky House.

HOUND HERO

A pair of robbers were stopped in their tracks by the brave and fearless Sausage!

Sausage captures burglars.

Hammy comes to stay.

·SCHOOL FOR DOGS·

Sausage starts school.

Now it is November, which means it is nearly… Sausage's BIRTHDAY!

"I have an idea," said Elly. "Let's have
a party for Sausage!"
"Good idea," said Jack and Gran.

"Woof, woof, wooooof!" said Sausage.
That is a sausagey way of saying,
"Yes, please!"

Chapter Two

"We can have balloons!" said Elly.
"And sausages," thought Sausage.

"Party food," said Elly.
"And sausages!" thought Sausage.

"We can have games!" said Jack.
"And sausages!" thought Sausage.

"And a cake," said Gran.
"With sausages?" thought Sausage.

"We can invite all Sausage's friends!" said Jack.
"We can make invitations... decorations... hats..." said Elly.

"... And, of course," said Gran, "we can have..."

Everyone was very excited.

Well… *nearly* everyone was very excited.
Fitz and Spatz, the snooty cats, were
not happy at all. They were jealous.
"All this fuss for one silly sausage
dog!" they said.
"It's not fair!" said Fitz.
"It's not right," said Spatz.
"And it's NOT going to happen,"
they both agreed.

Let's make a plan.

Chapter Three

Elly and Jack started to make the decorations and the invitations. Gran started planning the cake.

Sausage started choosing his birthday present. He looked through the *Party Animals* catalogue.

"That's what I want," he thought.

Fitz and Spatz started their skulking
and sulking and plotting and planning.
They were determined to find a way
of spoiling the party.

"We could pop all the balloons!" Fitz sniggered. He sharpened his razor claws.

"We could eat all his special cake!" Spatz licked his lips.

"I have a better idea," Fitz grinned. "Listen…"

"Hee hee! WICKED!" said Spatz.

Jack and Elly had a long list of Sausage's friends:

Spottydog

Dusty

Tiny

Scamp

Alfonso

Butch

Rex

Kevin

Lola

"They will all come to the party," said Elly. "Sausage is a very popular little dog."

Sausage smiled a little smile. It was a sausage-shaped smile.

Jack and Elly wrote out the invitations.

Please come to Sausage's party. Friday at 2 o'clock.

(Bring sausages!)

Proudly, Sausage added the final touch – his signature.

He took special care with Lola's invitation. And he put something extra on it – a great big red kiss.

Elly left all the invitations by the door. They were ready to be posted. Then she went to help with the other preparations. There was still a lot to do.

Chapter Four

Elly thought Gran had posted the invitations. Gran thought Jack had posted the invitations.

HAPPY BIRT

Jack thought Elly had posted the invitations. And Sausage thought *someone* had posted the invitations.

But here is what *really* happened...
Fitz and Spatz, the sneaky
cats, tiptoed into
the hall... grinned a
nasty grin... sniggered
a sneaky snigger...
whispered...

and then they pushed all the invitations into a bin bag. They dragged the bin bag outside and left it by the door, ready to be collected.

"Now no one will come to Sausage's party!" they said.

"It will be a total flop!" said Fitz.

"Hee! Hee! Wicked!" giggled Spatz.

Sausage thought his invitations were on their way. He imagined his friends being excited and looking forward to his party. His head was full of happy party thoughts.

Even the cats seemed happy. They each had a twinkle in their eyes and a funny little smile on their face. They seemed to be looking forward to the party, too.

The days passed slowly until, finally, it was…

PARTY DAY!

At two o'clock, Sausage stood by the window, waiting for his friends. He was looking forward to a brilliant party.

Time went on… and not one of his guests turned up. The only people who came to his street were the bin men coming to pick up the rubbish and the recycling.

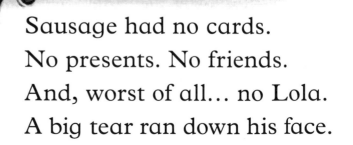

Sausage had no cards.
No presents. No friends.
And, worst of all… no Lola.
A big tear ran down his face.

Chapter Five

Outside in the street, the bin men continued with their work. Dan, the recycling man, was feeling a bit cross.

"So much MORE of this stuff could be recycled," he said.

He picked up a bin bag with a pile of letters in it and threw them into *his* truck.

"Woof!" agreed Dusty, his dog.

Suddenly, Dusty dived into the back of the truck and came out with a letter that was addressed to him.

"I never knew you could read, Dusty," said Dan.

"Who's a clever dog?"

"Look! This is an invitation. You're invited to a party... today!"

"Woof!" said Dusty.

He shook the dust from his paws and jumped down from the truck.

But Dan the recycling man stopped him. "No, Dusty," he said. "You can't go to the party… we have work to do."

Dusty and Dan got into the truck and drove away.

Chapter Six

All that afternoon, Sausage waited
and waited...

The two bad cats sniggered and sneered and sang a nasty song.

> Silly Sausage has no friends,
> Has no friends, has no friends,
> Silly Sausage has no friends,
> and he's NOT going to have
> a party!

Sausage was the saddest little sausage dog in the whole wide world.

And then… over the hill to the rescue came…

TA DA!

Dan the recycling man and his
not-so-dusty dog.

Dusty was all cleaned up and ready for the party and so were all the other dogs. Lola was looking particularly lovely.

"We found your invitations – and we delivered them," Dan explained. "We've brought your guests and we've brought you a present. Let the party begin!"

Chapter Seven

What a party! There was fine food to eat...

Hats to wear... → Dances to dance...

PIN THE TAIL ON THE DONKEY

There were games to play...

Songs to sing...

43

And, of course… presents! Sausage was given rubber balls, strings of sausages, a birthday jumper, a crunchy bone –

Bounce!

and the **big** bouncy birthday banana.

The cats sneered at the presents and tossed them to one side.

"What a load of rubbish!" they sneered.

Squeak!

Boing!

Squeak and BOING! went the bouncy banana as the bad cats flicked it across the room.

Then it was time for the cake.
Gran came in with it and everyone
started singing "Happy Birthday to You."

Then... it all went BANANAS!